This Boxer Books paperback belongs to

. . . .

www.boxerbooks.com

For Frances and Jessie Wardlaw. Much love, C.M. xxx
And with special thanks to Fran Elks.

First published in hardback in Great Britain in 2011 by Boxer Books Limited.
First published in paperback in Great Britain in 2012 by Boxer Books Limited.
www.boxerbooks.com

Text and illustrations copyright © 2011 Cathy MacLennan

The right of Cathy MacLennan to be identified as the author and
illustrator of this work has been asserted by her
in accordance with the Copyright, Designs and Patents Act, 1988.

The illustrations were prepared using acrylic paints on brown kraft paper.
The text is set in Hoefler.

ISBN 978-1-907967-25-2

1 3 5 7 9 10 8 6 4 2

Printed in China.

All of our papers are sourced from managed forests and renewable resources.

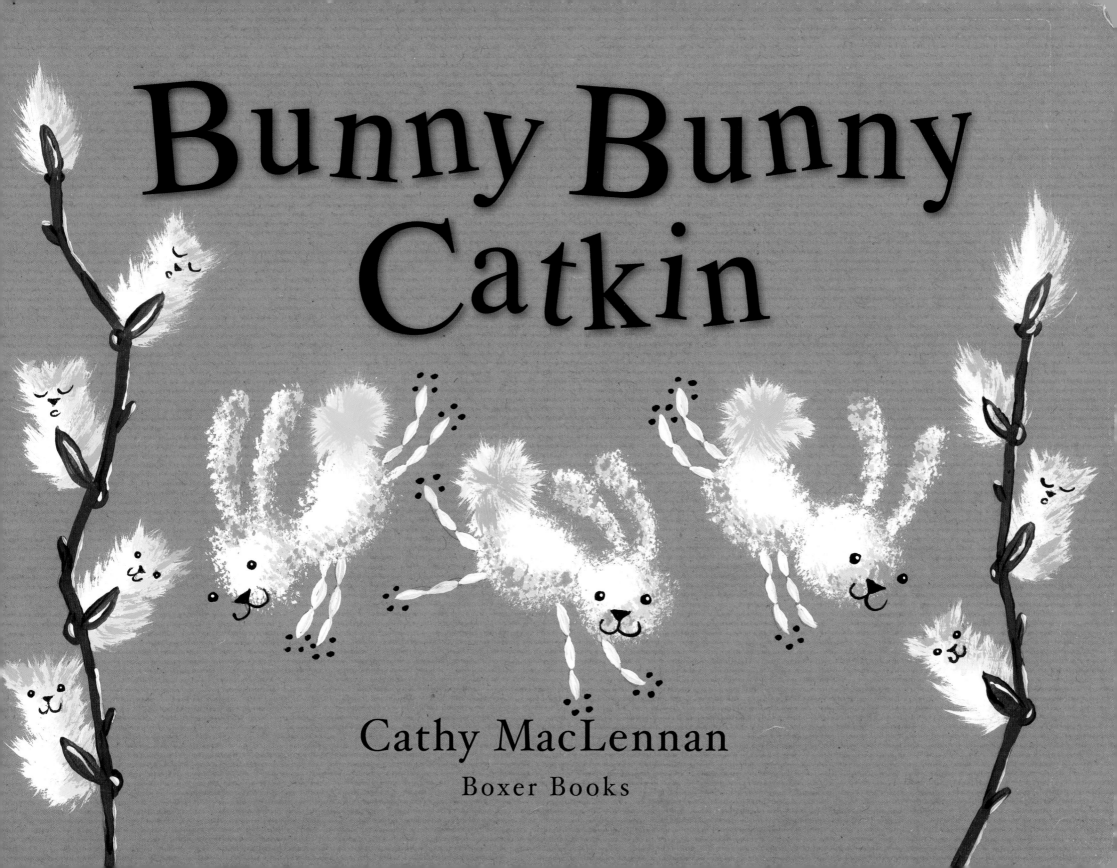

Bunny Bunny Catkin

Cathy MacLennan

Boxer Books

Soft, soft rays of
warm, warm sun,
sweet drip-drops of rain.
No more quiver, quiver,
no more shake and shiver.

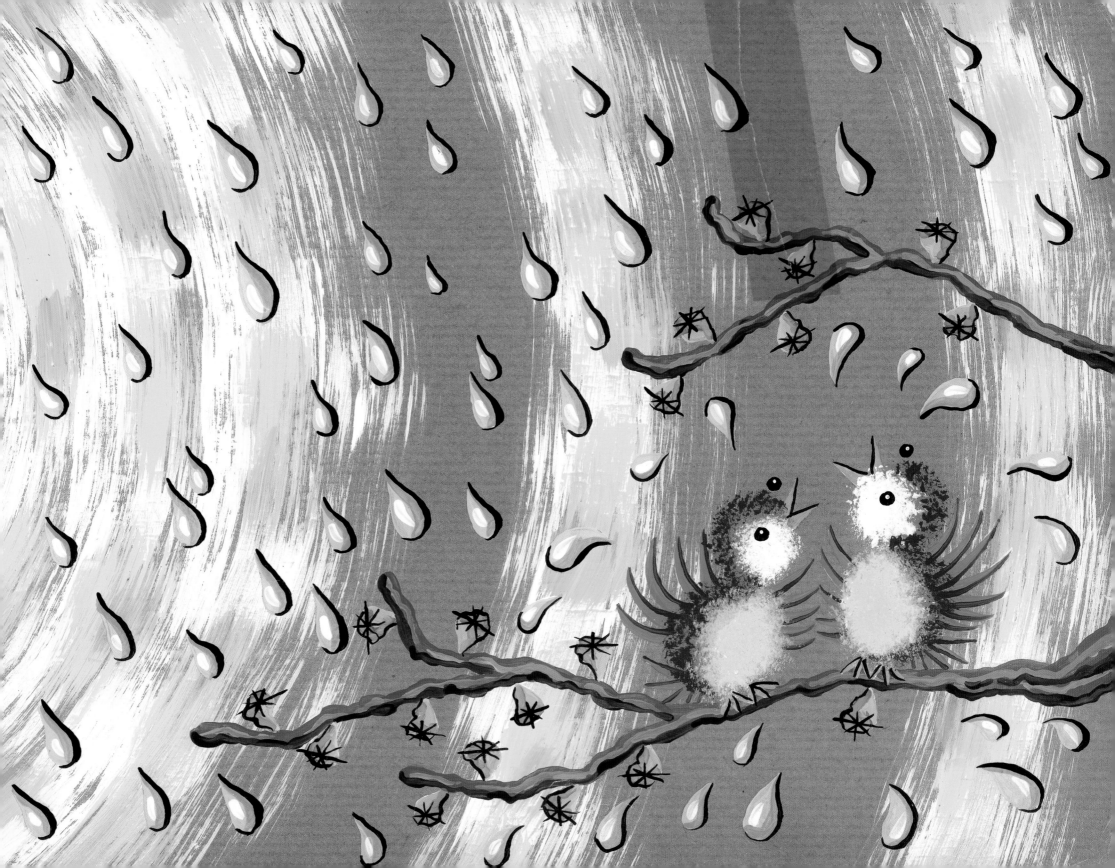

It's time! It's time!
It's time to rise and

Bunny, bunny catkin, catkin, catkin.

Bunnies, bunnies hopping,
hopping, hopping.
Funny bunny catkins,

hop,

hop,

hop!

Kitty, kitty catkin,
catkin, catkin.
Kitties, kitties peeking,
peeking, peeking.
Kitty, kitty
catkins . . .
in a
kitten tree!

Birdy, birdy,
blossom,
blossom,
blossom.

Birdies, birdies,
building,
twigs and blossom.

Baby birdies tweeting,
chirping,
chirping.
Baby birdies
nestling . . .
in a
blossom-ball!

Caterpillar, caterpillar,

crawling, climbing.

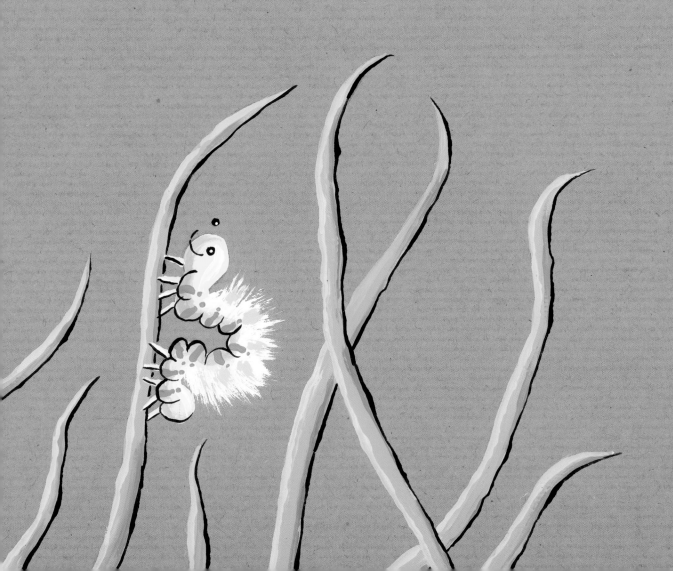

Caterpillar,
caterpillar,
green
grass
growing.

Caterpillars, caterpillars, munching, lunching.

Lots of little caterpillars,
wriggling, squiggling,
in a green-grass carpet!

Longer days . . .
then brighter days.
Mellow, yellow sun rays.

Now what is that,

Blossom in the breezes,
and tickly, tickly sneezes.

that we can see?

Fluffy, yellow catkins,
and furry bunnies

hopping.

Caterpillars fluttering and baby birds a-flying.

Spring,

spring,

spring has...

unng!

More Boxer Books paperbacks to enjoy

Chicky Chicky Chook Chook • Cathy MacLennan

A great read-aloud, sing-along book, full of fun-to-imitate animal sounds, rhythm and movement. Chicky chicks, buzzy bees and kitty cats romp in the sun and snuggle in the warmth until, pitter-patter, down comes the rain. A fun onomatopoeic text with a beautiful and unique art style.
'Lovely to read aloud.' The Times

ISBN 978-1-905417-32-2

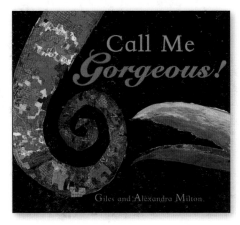

Call Me Gorgeous! • Giles Milton & Alexandra Milton

Discover a mysterious and fabulous creature in this beautiful book from Giles and Alexandra Milton. It has a porcupine's spines and a crocodile's teeth, a chameleon's tail and a cockerel's feet. What on earth could it be?

ISBN 978-1-907152-49-8

Toot Toot Beep Beep • Emma Garcia

Toot Toot Beep Beep is a fun, bright book for young children. Colourful cars zoom across the page, each making their own special noise. Little ones will love joining in with the sounds, making this book perfect for reading aloud. *Toot Toot Beep Beep* is the follow-up to the highly successful *Tip Tip Dig Dig*, which was shortlisted for the Read It Again! Picture Book Award for an outstanding debut picture book.

ISBN 978-1-906250-51-5

The Art of Storytelling

www.boxerbooks.com